P9-BXW-969

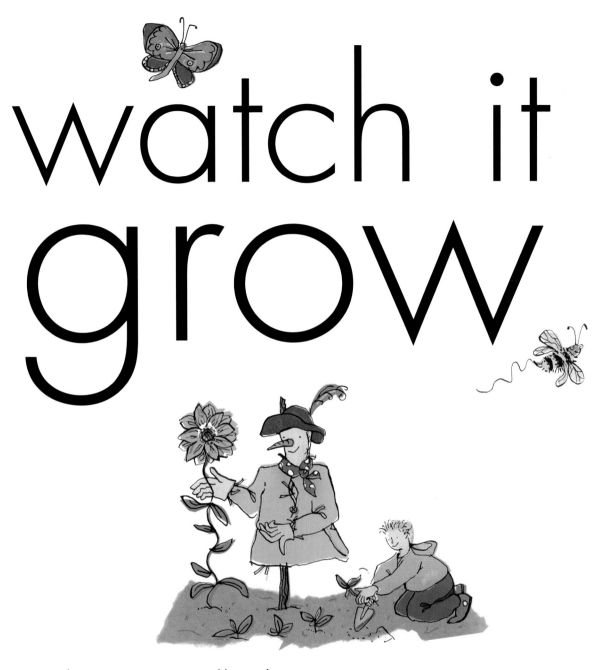

watch it grow

by Ivan Bulloch & Diane James

Photography by Daniel Pangbourne

Illustrations by Emily Hare

TWO-CAN™

PRINCETON ■ LONDON

www.two-canpublishing.com

Published in the United States and Canada by
Two-Can Publishing LLC
234 Nassau Street
Princeton, NJ 08542

Copyright © 2001, 1998 Two-Can Publishing

For information on Two-Can books and multimedia,
call 1-609-921-6700, fax 1-609-921-3349, or visit our Web site at
http://www.two-canpublishing.com

Created by
act-two
346 Old Street
London EC1V 9RB

Art Director Ivan Bulloch
Editor Diane James
Design Assistant David Oh
Editorial Assistant Katherine Harvey
Gardening Consultant Sue Hook
U.S. Editor Karen Ingebretsen

With thanks to Jimmy and Winsome James for letting us use their garden
and also Jackie Hyde, Sue Gibbs, Nicky, Katie, George, and Sam

hc ISBN: 1-58728-500-2
sc ISBN: 1-58728-501-0
LC: 97-62334

hc 1 2 3 4 5 6 7 8 9 10 02 01
sc 1 2 3 4 5 6 7 8 9 10 02 01

Printed in Hong Kong

contents

watch it grow

Gardening is great fun! It also takes some work and patience, but the results are worth it. Even a beginner can grow colorful, healthy plants.

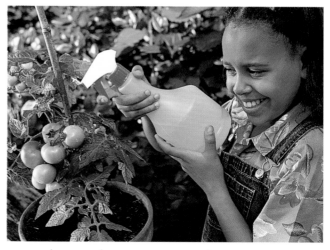

You can learn a lot about gardening just chatting with friends who garden. You can also get ideas by looking at books on gardening, exploring other gardens, and visiting garden centers. The scarecrow in this book has plenty of good advice, too!

Work, watch, and enjoy.

Once you start growing your own plants, you won't want to stop. It's a great way to enjoy the outdoors.

Have fun!

getting started

Plants are living things. Just like people they come in lots of different shapes and sizes. Some plants can survive cold, windy conditions. Others need warmth and shelter. All plants need light, food, air, and water. They benefit by being looked after, too!

Before you begin gardening, here are some things you need to know.

flower
leaf
stem
root

Growing up Nearly all plants grow from either seeds or bulbs. Each seed contains enough food for a plant to start growing, but the seed also needs soil and water. When you plant a seed in soil, it grows roots that push downward. The roots anchor the plant in the soil and take in water and food from it. The seed pushes a stem and leaves above the soil. The leaves use sunlight and carbon dioxide (a gas in the air) to make food to help the plant grow.

Now or later You can start your garden with seeds, bulbs, or ready-made plants. Growing plants from seeds takes a little longer, but it's really fun to watch the sprouts come up! Bulbs must be planted in fall for a colorful show of flowers in spring.

These bulbs will make a colorful display when it is too cold for other plants to grow.

Color and space There is a huge range of plants to choose from. Think about colors, shapes, and which ones will look good together. You should also keep in mind how much space you have!

Annuals These are plants that "visit" the garden. They are easy to grow from seeds, but they die in the same year. You'll find lots of annuals in garden centers as ready-to-grow plants.

Brightly colored annuals look good in pots and window boxes.

Trees are the tallest plants. They provide shade and shelter for all kinds of animals. This apple tree will also provide delicious fruit that you can eat.

Biennials These grow from seeds into young plants one year, then flower and die the following year.

Perennials These flowering plants grow from seeds and come up year after year. They disappear in winter but shoot up again when the weather warms up in spring.

Bulbs A bulb has layers of fleshy leaves which contain food for the growing plant. Some bulbs push strong, green shoots above the soil even in cold, frosty weather.

Shrubs You can recognize a shrub by its woody stems and chunky shape. The plant on the right is a small shrub.

Trees These giants of the plant world live longer than anything else in the garden. They need a lot of space for their long, strong roots and branches to spread out.

tips and tools

When you start gardening, you'll only need a few basic tools. You can get more equipment as your garden grows bigger! Good tools will last for years if you take care of them. Be very careful of sharp edges!

Watering can This is important, especially during dry weather. Plants need a good soaking, not a sprinkle, to keep them from drooping! Watering cans have a spray attachment over the spout so that the water showers out gently. In a large garden, use a hose to water in early morning or early evening. Collect rain water in a bucket.

Trowel Use a trowel for digging in small spaces, such as pots and window boxes. A trowel can also be used to dig out the roots of stubborn weeds in the garden.

Rake Use this to level the soil, comb off stones, and break up the surface into fine crumbs. A rake with long, thin prongs is good for scraping leaves from the lawn.

Trays, pots, and labels
Use seed trays to grow plants from seeds. Small pots are useful for seedlings or cuttings before they are planted in the garden. Use labels if you think you might forget what you have planted!

Fork A small fork will help with the same jobs as a trowel, especially weeding. Use it to break up the soil, too.

Sticks Use long wooden or bamboo sticks to keep tall plants upright. Poke one into the soil next to the plant and tie the stem of the plant to it.

Tie it up Support plants by tying them to sticks with soft string or garden twine.

Never eat anything from the garden without asking a grown-up first! Many plants are poisonous.

These berries are for animals only!

Spade A spade with a long handle is best for turning soil over to break up lumps. It is also useful for digging large holes to plant trees and shrubs. Clean your spade and all your garden tools before you put them away.

More care, less speed Don't rush jobs in the garden. Take your time or you may damage plants and even yourself. Try to finish one job before you start the next.

Clothes Gardening clothes should be comfortable and practical. Gardening gloves will help stop blisters and cuts. Always wash your hands after gardening.

9

seed sowing

Growing your own plants from seeds is extremely satisfying! Sow seeds by scattering them over your planting area and covering them lightly with soil. If you live in a cool climate, sow seeds indoors to give them a head start. Wait until the danger of frost is past before planting the seedlings outdoors. Tender young plants won't survive the cold!

> It's best to sow seeds thinly.

> If you don't, the plants will grow much too close together.

Seed trays Buy plastic seed trays, or make holes in the bottom of empty food containers and egg cartons. You can put your trays on a windowsill indoors, or in a cold frame in the garden. Some trays are sold with protective covers.

Patience! It may be several weeks before you see the seedlings appear, although some seeds sprout very quickly. Check them daily. Make sure that the soil is moist and the trays are not in direct sunlight. Some seeds need darkness to sprout. If you have put a protective cover over the seeds, take it off when you see the first green seedlings.

Indoors or outdoors? Some seeds can be sown outdoors. Make sure you prepare their space first. Dig and rake the soil to get rid of lumps and stones and to make a level surface.

how to do it

1 Fill a seed tray almost to the top with potting soil and level the surface. Water the soil using a watering can with a spray attachment.

2 Sprinkle the seeds on the surface. Cover them with a thin layer of soil. Use a spray to moisten the soil without disturbing the seeds.

Growing bigger! Keep a careful eye on your new seedlings. Don't let the soil dry out. Turn to the next page to find out what to do next.

Soil for seeds Use potting soil or a special seed-starting mixture, which you can buy at garden centers. These have all the food your seeds need to start them off. It's like buying special food for babies!

3 Cover the seed tray with a clear cover or plastic wrap to protect the seeds. Put the tray in a warm, lighted place. Label the tray.

moving on

When your seeds have pushed their way up through the soil and grown leaves, they are called seedlings.

Now they need more space to grow. Moving seedlings to a new home is called pricking out. Treat them carefully and your seedlings will grow into strong, healthy plants. Give any spare seedlings to your friends.

1 Fill a seed tray, or pots, with potting soil. Water the tray and level the surface. Use a plastic plant label or a wooden ice-cream stick, to help separate out a small clump of seedlings from the rest. Hold the leaves of one seedling and gently pull it away from the others.

Time to move Check your trays every day. The first two leaves that a seedling grows are called "seed" leaves. Don't be surprised; the next set of leaves will look quite different! When these "true" leaves appear on the seedlings, it's time to prick them out.

2 Make a small hole in the soil with the plant label or stick. Put the seedling in and firm the soil around it. Give each seedling's roots plenty of room. Now water the trays and pots using a fine spray attachment.

Weather watch! In late spring when the weather is warm and there is no frost, you can put your pricked-out seedlings outside for a few hours during the day. This is called "hardening off" and it prepares the seedlings for being planted in the garden.

Planting outdoors Treat seedlings bought from a garden center in the same way as seedlings you have grown. Prepare the soil by breaking up lumps with a fork. Pull any weeds, then rake the surface to even it out. Make a hole large enough for each new plant. Support the plant with both hands, then put it into the hole. Push soil gently around the plant, then water.

Give each new plant plenty of space to grow upward and spread outward.

Don't plant your seedlings outdoors too soon. Wait until they have strong roots.

Check the packet to find out how tall your plants will grow.

Put tall plants toward the back of the flower bed.

13

planting bulbs

One of the best known bulbs is the onion we eat! Lots of flowering plants also grow from bulbs. Favorites are the brave, colorful bulbs that push their way through frosty ground to let us know that warmer weather is on its way! You can grow bulbs in flower beds or containers. Some bulbs are happy to grow indoors.

Look for bulbs that are heavy, solid, and not badly marked or moldy.

When to plant? The best time to plant most bulbs is in the fall. Many bulbs don't like being out of soil for long periods, so try to buy them when you have time to plant them right away.

Top and bottom Sometimes it is tricky to tell which way is up when planting a bulb. Usually, the pointed end produces the growing shoot and the flat end produces the roots. With small bulbs you may not be able to tell the difference. If in doubt, plant the bulb on its side. As a general rule, plant bulbs twice as deep as their height.

It is easy to see the roots on this bulb!

14

Leave your bulbs in the ground and they will spread and come up year after year.

Bulb planter This is a special tool to help you plant bulbs, especially if you want them to push up through your lawn. Use it to remove a small, circular plug of soil and turf. Plant the bulb in the hole and replace the turf.

Next year's food When a bulb has finished flowering, don't cut back straggly leaves. Be patient and wait until they go brown. The bulb's leaves make food for the next year's growth.

Where did I put it? Label your bulbs as soon as you have planted them. That way, you won't forget and dig them up before the leaves and flowers appear above the soil.

how to do it

1 Plant a container with bulbs to make a colorful spring display on an outdoor windowsill or patio. Put small pebbles in the bottom to help water drain.

2 Half fill the container with a rich potting soil. Place the bulbs, root sides down, on top of the soil. Put them close together, but not touching.

3 Cover the bulbs with more soil. Some can have their tips showing. Make sure the soil is moist but not soggy, or the bulbs will rot.

15

keep at it!

After you have planted your seeds, bulbs, and new plants, there's still plenty to do to help your plants grow strong, healthy, and beautiful. Try to do one or two chores in the garden each day, so the work doesn't pile up.

Save water! Collect rain water in buckets and use it to give your thirsty plants a drink.

Thirsty work On hot, sunny days, the soil soon dries out and plants need a drink. Nothing is as good as a shower of rain, but you can help. Wait until early evening and give everything a good soaking. Direct the water at the bottom of plants so that you don't waste it and damage flower heads. Remember the plants in pots, too!

Look out! When you are doing different jobs in the garden, keep an eye out for damage caused by garden pests. Look for tell-tale holes in leaves, discolored leaves, and droopy plants. Can you see what is causing the damage? You'll find some tips to help you deal with troublemakers on pages 22 and 23.

Use a hose for large flower beds and lawns, and a watering can for small areas.

Tie plants up carefully. Very tall plants will need securing in several places.

Stand up! Tall plants with heavy blooms will droop if you don't give them support. Before they grow tall, poke a stick into the soil beside each plant. Tie the stem to the stick.

Spick-and-span General jobs include raking up dead leaves and keeping borders neat and tidy. Deadheading is also important. This means cutting off flower heads when they have finished flowering. It encourages more flowers to grow.

Weed it out A weed is any plant growing where you don't want it. Some plants have long, spreading roots which take food away from other plants. Some even wrap themselves around other plants, eventually strangling them. Make sure you get rid of all the roots of an unwanted weed. If you don't, before you know it, the weed will grow back again.

If you've got a big garden, share the jobs with friends who like gardening!

All year long There always seem to be more jobs in the summer when the garden is in full bloom. Tidying up and keeping an eye on things is important, even in winter when there is not much growing.

Dig around weeds and pull them up gently with their roots. You may have to dig deep.

plants to eat

 There is nothing more delicious than eating home-grown vegetables and fruit. You don't need a lot of space to grow plants to eat. Many will be quite happy in containers. When the weather is sunny and there is no danger of frost, try growing some tasty pole beans in a big pot.

1 Make a teepee for your pole beans in a large pot or in the garden. Push three sticks into the soil and tie them at the top to make a pyramid. Plant a bean seed, or small plant, at the bottom of each stick.

2 As the plants climb, wind them around each stick. After a few months, you will see red flowers which will turn into beans. When the beans are about 4 inches (10 cm) long, they are ready to be picked.

18

Tomatoes need lots of water, especially on sunny days. When the fruits appear, give them plant food (see page 25).

The fruits can become heavy. Support your tomato plant by tying it in different places to one or more sticks.

Pick the fruits as soon as they are ripe. Wash them and eat them right away to get the best taste!

Ready to eat? The parts of vegetables that you eat can grow above or below the soil. Test vegetables growing underground by digging one up. Tiny carrots taste sweet and delicious. Don't let them grow big and woody.

A whole meal! Vegetables are delicious and easy to grow. Think about what you like to eat in your salad. How about lettuce, tomatoes, zucchini, radishes, and carrots? Buy seed packets for your favorite veggies. Start sowing in spring for tasty and healthy treats in summer!

Always fresh Vegetables and fruits grow at different times of the year. Some, such as beans and tomatoes, prefer warm, sunny weather. Others, like potatoes, can brave winter frosts. Work out a timetable using the information on seed packets, and you will have something fresh every day.

Protect young vegetable plants or the birds will eat them!

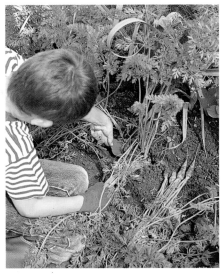

Dig up root vegetables carefully so that you don't damage them. If you are left with too many vegetables, don't forget your friends and neighbors.

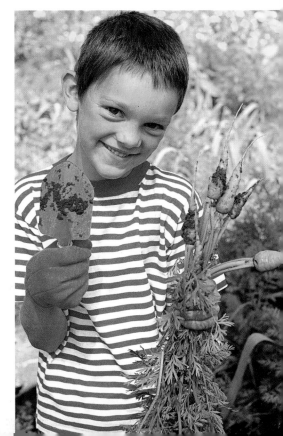

herbs

Herbs are another kind of plant you can eat. They add amazing flavor to your cooking and to salads. Herbs often taste and smell quite strong, so you only need to use a few leaves at a time. For hundreds of years, people have used herbs as a cure for different illnesses – from colds and headaches to bruises and tummy aches. They are good-looking plants, too. Always ask a grown-up to tell you if an herb is safe to eat.

Happy together Many herbs grow well in dry, stony soil. Choose a sunny patch of ground, or a large pot, and plant a selection of herbs. Traditional herb gardens are often planted so that the herbs grow in patterns. Herbs can be planted in an area on their own, or in flower beds with other plants.

Stop your herbs from growing straggly.

Pinch off the tops of the growing shoots.

All year long To make sure you have fresh herbs in the winter, sow seeds in small pots toward the end of summer. Keep them on the kitchen windowsill and snip leaves off when you need them. For an even bigger supply, harvest herbs from the garden and dry them.

1 Try drying herbs so you have a supply over winter. Pick bunches of your favorite herbs and rinse thoroughly. Tie them with garden twine or raffia. Remove leaves that are damaged or discolored.

2 Hang the bunches in a dry, airy room, such as a pantry or closet, and leave them for a couple of weeks. When the herbs are completely dry, they will feel slightly crackly.

Tastes good! Try experimenting by adding herbs to food to find out which flavors you like best. Chopping or tearing fresh herbs into small pieces releases the flavor and makes it easy to scatter them evenly.

3 Take the dry leaves off the stems and rub them into tiny pieces. Put them in clean, dry jars with screw-on tops. Label each jar. Dry herbs taste stronger than fresh ones, so you don't need to use as much of them.

know your friends

Gardens are full of other living things besides plants! It's good to know which creatures to encourage to share your garden, and which ones may damage your plants. A bit of detective work will sort out the good guys from the bad ones!

Worms are a gardener's best friend. They work day and night to enrich the soil.

Slugs and snails These slippery creatures love to feed on plants and can do a lot of damage. The best way to stop them is to put up barriers. You can protect young plants by surrounding them with a collar cut from a plastic bottle. Or, cover the surface of the soil around the plant with broken eggshells. Keep a special eye on young seedlings.

Grow plants that provide food for insects such as butterflies.

Making seeds Flowers must be pollinated before they can make new seeds, which in turn grow into new plants. Insects carry a special powder found in plants, called pollen, from one flower to another. The patterns on flower petals guide the insects to the pollen, which is in the middle of the flower. Pollen carriers are important. Look out for bees with thick powder on their legs!

Friends Ladybugs, hedgehogs, frogs, and toads all feed on harmful insects and will not damage your plants.

Slugs and snails hate crawling over anything prickly or sharp – like eggshells!

22

how to do it

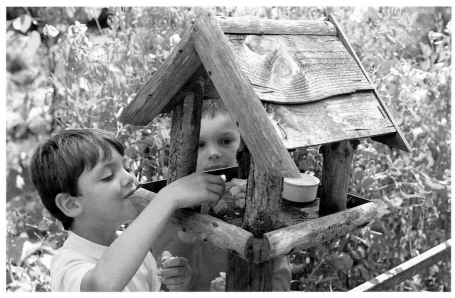

Don't forget that birds need water as well as food. They need your help most in the cold winter months when they cannot find their favorite meal of worms and insects.

1 Pests love to hide in dark places. Keep your garden clean and tidy. Don't leave piles of leaves, bits of wood, or stacks of old flowerpots where pests can hide and multiply.

Feathered friends No garden is complete without the sound of birds chirping, but you may have to put up with a bit of damage! Birds like to nibble young shoots and buds. In return, they are happy to gobble up snails, as well as slugs, caterpillars, and other bugs that may damage your plants.

Spraying Think twice before using a chemical spray to get rid of pests. You may harm some of the creatures that your garden needs. Spray the culprits with soapy water, or pick them off the plants by hand. If you spot the problem soon enough, you can act before the bugs eat your plants.

2 Prop up an empty grapefruit half with a small stone. Slugs will shelter under it. Pick up the grapefruit with the slugs inside and put it out of harm's way!

3 Look for caterpillars on leaves. Lift them off gently with your fingers and put them where they can't do any damage!

Give plants a soapy soaking, paying attention to the undersides of the leaves.

planting in pots

You don't need to have a large space to enjoy growing plants! Pots and tubs come in many different shapes and sizes and will fit into all sorts of spaces.

What to plant Most plants – from a tiny herb to a bushy shrub – will grow in a container. Find out how tall and wide each plant will grow, and choose a big enough pot. Try growing different kinds of plants in the same pot.

What kind of pot The ideal pot is waterproof and will stand firmly on the ground without wobbling. It should have at least one hole in the bottom to allow water to drain through. Most plants do not like to grow in waterlogged soil.

Looking after pots Plants growing in pots need the same amount of care as plants growing in the garden. Make sure the soil does not dry out, and check for pests! Look out for nipped-off buds and holes in leaves.

Use a large can to make an instant container. Ask a grown-up to punch drainage holes in the bottom. Don't try to do it yourself!

Plants in pots need watering more often than those in the garden!

Grouping Think about the best way to display your flower pots. Try having one large central pot and surrounding it with smaller ones. What about several single flower pots in a row, perhaps on a window ledge?

Feed me Because potted plants grow in less soil than those in the garden, they sometimes need extra help to keep them growing. You can buy special plant food in garden centers to give your plants when you are watering. Make sure you follow the instructions on the package.

how to do it

1 Put some pieces of broken flower pots, or a layer of gravel, in the bottom of the container to improve drainage. Pour in soil about halfway for large plants and higher for small ones. Place the pot on an old saucer or plant tray.

2 Gently separate the roots of the plants and place them in position. Use a trowel to fill in the soil around the plants and gently press the soil down around the plant. Leave a small space at the top of the container. Now water your plants well.

Bold and bright arrangements are colorful and eye-catching. Pale and dark shades of one color look calm and peaceful.

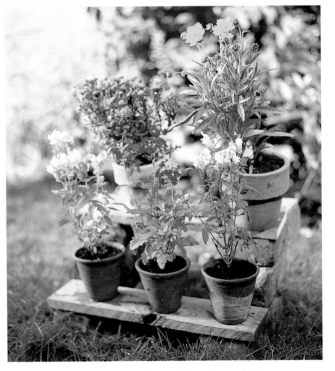

Two planks of wood and a few bricks make a platform to display pots at different heights. It also saves on space!

free plants!

You don't have to spend a lot of money to garden! Many plants can be grown from cuttings. With care, and luck, you can take a piece of an adult plant and grow a new one from it. Shrubs and trees grow much quicker from cuttings than from seed. You can also collect and grow seeds from plants that have finished flowering, or from fruit you have eaten.

Hit and miss Don't be upset if some of your cuttings don't grow. Take about twice as many cuttings as you need and you will end up with plenty of plants – and probably some to spare!

Swap seeds and cuttings with your friends.

Hard and soft Soft cuttings are taken in early summer from young, fleshy shoots. Hard cuttings are taken in autumn from older, woody stems. An easy method is known as a heel cutting. Choose a healthy looking side shoot – hard or soft without flowers – and pull it downward, away from the main stem. The extra bit left at the bottom looks a bit like a heel.

Full speed ahead You can take cuttings in early summer or in autumn. Gather your cuttings as quickly as possible and pop them in a plastic bag to protect them. Plant your cuttings right away.

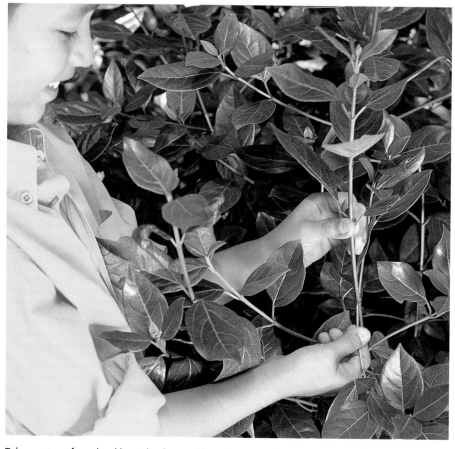

Take cuttings from healthy side shoots. Plant them in soil as soon as possible.

1 Fill small flowerpots nearly to the top with potting soil. Water them well. Use the end of a pencil to make a small hole for each cutting. Strip the bottom leaves off the cutting and poke it into the hole. Firm the soil around the stem.

2 You can put more than one cutting in each pot, but make sure they have plenty of space. Tie a clear plastic bag over the pot, or use an upturned jelly jar, taking care not to touch the cuttings. This will help to keep the soil moist.

3 Put the pot out of direct sunlight. Keep the soil damp, not soggy. After two or three weeks, take the bag off and keep an eye on your new plants. Outdoor cuttings can be planted in the garden when they have strong roots.

Give it a try! Some cuttings will grow from a single leaf and its stem. Choose a plant with a large, healthy leaf like the one below. Cut off a single leaf with a bit of stem. Poke the stem into a pot of potting soil. If you are lucky, after about a month you will see a new plant growing from the bottom of the leaf.

A quick drink Another way to try your luck is to pop a cutting into a glass of water. Keep the glass in a lighted place and watch to see if roots grow from the sides of the submerged stem. If they do, plant the cutting in a pot of soil as you did before.

Seed bank Another way to save money is to collect seeds from dry flower seed heads in late summer. Keep them in a labeled paper bag and sow them in spring.

27

a perfect bunch

Picking flowers and leafy stems from the garden and making them into a colorful arrangement can really cheer up a room – they often smell lovely, too! A bunch of cut flowers makes a good present, especially if you have grown them yourself.

Try to keep flowers away from the hot sun when you have picked them.

Don't pick wild flowers in the country.

They are for everyone to enjoy.

What color? It's best to have a plan before you start picking flowers. Look around to see what is available and decide which colors you like best.

Don't pick all the flowers in the garden. Leave some so that you can enjoy them indoors *and* outdoors!

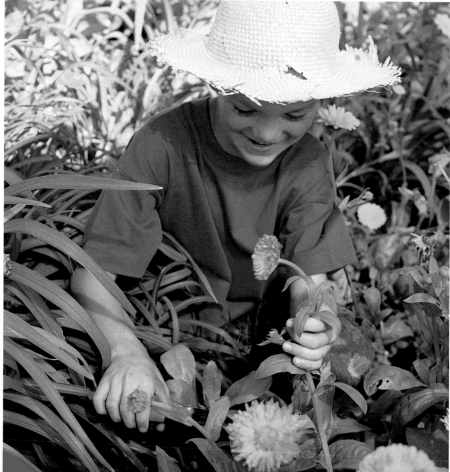

Pick the best Look for flowers that are about to bloom. They will last longer when you take them indoors. Use a pair of scissors to cut the flower stems close to the bottom. Try to put the cut flowers in water as soon as possible.

The right vase You can use any container for a flower arrangement, as long as it is waterproof. A simple jelly jar, a small bucket, or even an old teapot all work well.

Keep still! Here are a few tricks to keep your arrangement in place. You can buy a special type of foam from flower shops. Cut it to fit the bottom of your vase and fill the vase with water. Push the flower stems into the wet foam. Another method of keeping stems in place is to fill the bottom of the vase with marbles before poking in the flower stems.

Find a container in a color that will look good with your flower colors and you can't go wrong!

1 Choose a tall vase for long stems or a small one for short stems. Put a piece of foam or some marbles in the bottom. Fill the vase with water.

2 Start with the longest stems and push them into the middle. Then fill in around the edges with the shorter stems.

Longer lasting To keep your arrangement fresh for as long as possible, strip the bottom leaves off the stems before you put them in water. If you don't, they will rot and the flowers will die. Take out single stems as they die off. Change the water every day.

indoor plants

Growing plants indoors is just as satisfying as growing them in the garden. Garden centers and supermarkets sell indoor plants. Read the instructions on the plant label to find out how to take care of your new plant. Be careful when choosing your indoor plants. Some are poisonous to pets.

When you go on vacation, give your indoor plants to a friend for safe keeping.

Not too much! Indoor plants need watering just like those outside, but not too much. Water them about once a week in summer and less in winter when they are not growing. Put your pots on saucers, or in a bowl slightly larger than the pot. Don't leave plants sitting in water.

The best place Indoor plants like light, but not direct sunlight, which will burn their leaves and dry out the soil. Don't put your plants in a drafty place.

All sizes You can buy plants to suit any space – small plants for narrow windowsills or huge ones to brighten a dark corner. Try grouping plants together to make a colorful display.

1 Don't let your plants become dusty! Gently brush leaves with a soft brush. You can buy leaf shine wipes, which are useful for cleaning big, waxy leaves.

2 Use a water spray to perk up your plants during hot weather. Spray a fine mist onto the leaves, but don't spray the furniture!

Summer holiday On hot, sunny days, most indoor plants enjoy spending time outside. Prickly cacti are especially fond of sunny days, probably because they are most at home in the desert! Handle them carefully.

index

a

annual 7

b

bamboo sticks 9
bees 22
biennial 7
birds 23
bucket 8
bulb 6, 7, 14-15
butterflies 22

c

cactus 31
carrots 19
caterpillars 23
cuttings 8, 26-27

f

flower arranging 28-29
fork 8, 13
frogs 22

h

hedgehogs 22
herbs 20-21, 24
hose 8, 16
house plants 30-31

l

ladybugs 22
lettuce 19

o

onions 14

p

perennial 7
pests 16, 22-23, 24
plant food 19, 25
pole beans 18
pollination 22
potatoes 19
pots 7, 8, 12, 18, 20, 24-25, 27, 30

r

radishes 19
rake 8, 17
roots 6, 7, 12, 13, 14, 15, 25, 27

s

seed 6, 7, 10-11, 19, 20, 22, 26, 27
seedling 8, 10, 11, 12-13
shrub 7, 9, 24, 26
slugs 22, 23
snails 22, 23
spade 9

t

toads 22
tomatoes 19
tree 7, 9, 26
trowel 8, 25
twine 9

w

watering 8, 11, 16, 24, 25, 30
weeds 8, 13, 17
window box 7, 8, 15